Who You Are

Written by: Jessi Hersey
Illustrated by: Lizaveta Tararuk

Written by: Jessi Hersey

Illustrated by: Lizaveta Tararuk

To all the children that read this book series:

◇◇

I want to thank my little readers for taking the time to read and enjoy the pages of this book. I would like to thank my friends and family, who have always been there for me. Thank you to my close friends—you know who you are—for simply being fans of my writing and supporting me as I follow my heart and pursue my writing fromscratch all over again.

I want to give a shout out to my Mom, Dad, and Katy Vargo for being there for me and being huge supporters of me as a person for who I truly am. Thank you for being some of the biggest fans of my writing, which all comes from the heart. I would like to thank God for giving me the inspiration for this entire new idea to write a series of children's books, which only continues to grow. I look forward to seeing this new journey to its beginning!

Meet Jaylin. She feels like she is supposed to be the person that everyone is telling her to be.

Don't let anyone tell you who to be!

Instead, follow your heart and let it be.

The ones who are true
will love you for you.

Find yourself in everything you do.

Passion and joy come naturally once you find what brings life to you, whether it be:

Writing

Singing

Dancing

Swinging

Helping others

Painting

Cheering

Counseling

Studying

Hiking

Biking

Planting

RESCUING

Praying

Playing

Studying a new language

Aimez-vous étudier?

Jumping rope

Catching frogs

Playing video games

Watching favorite show

Follow your heart to discover who you truly are.

The beginning

Follow on Social media

Instagram: @Jessistories

Twitter: @Jessistories

The company Facebook page: @Onenesslovepublishing

Twitch: twitch.tv/jessistories

Instagram: 1nesslove123

Children's book Facebook page: @whoyouare

Poetry Book Facebook page: @litsoul77

You can explore services in coaching in publishing here: www.1nesslove.com

Made in the USA
Las Vegas, NV
08 November 2021